YEA

GREENWICKS

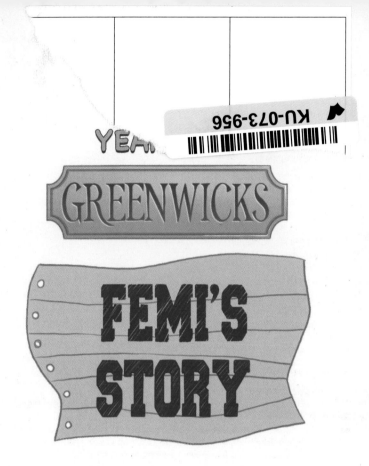

FEMI'S STORY

Written by Adam and Charlotte Guillain
Illustrated by Katie Kear

RISING ★ STARS

With thanks to The MS Society for their input. For information and support for anyone with MS, or their family and friends. Call our free MS Helpline on 0808 800 8000 or visit mssociety.org.uk

Hachette UK's policy is to use papers that are natural, renewable and recyclable products and made from wood grown in well-managed forests and other controlled sources. The logging and manufacturing processes are expected to conform to the environmental regulations of the country of origin.

ISBN: 9781398324312

Text © Adam and Charlotte Guillain
Illustrations, design and layout © Hodder and Stoughton Ltd
First published in 2022 by Hodder & Stoughton Limited (for its Rising Stars imprint, part of the Hodder Education Group),
An Hachette UK Company
Carmelite House 50 Victoria Embankment London EC4Y 0DZ
www.risingstars-uk.com

Impression number 10 9 8 7 6 5 4 3 2 1
Year 2026 2025 2024 2023 2022

Author: Adam and Charlotte Guillain
Series Editor: Tony Bradman
Commissioning Editor: Hamish Baxter
Illustrator: Katie Kear/Bright International Group
Educational Reviewer: Helen Marron
Design concept: David Bates
Page layouts: Rocket Design (East Anglia) Ltd
Editor: Amy Tyrer

With thanks to the schools that took part in the development of *Reading Planet* KS2, including: Ancaster CE Primary School, Ancaster; Downsway Primary School, Reading; Ferry Lane Primary School, London; Foxborough Primary School, Slough; Griffin Park Primary School, Blackburn; St Barnabas CE First & Middle School, Pershore; Tranmoor Primary School, Doncaster; and Wilton CE Primary School, Wilton.

A catalogue record for this title is available from the British Library.

Printed in the United Kingdom

Orders: Please contact Hachette UK Distribution, Hely Hutchinson Centre, Milton Road, Didcot, Oxfordshire, OX11 7HH.

Telephone: (44) 01235 400555. Email: primary@hachette.co.uk.

MIX
Paper from
responsible sources
FSC™ C104740

Contents

1 What's Up with Femi?

"I'm getting myself some breakfast," Femi called up the stairs.

Femi's mum had shouted down to remind him to eat breakfast while he was putting out the rubbish, but she didn't have to worry. There was one thing Femi had become brilliant at over the last year – fitting things in.

Femi yawned as he popped two pieces of bread into the toaster and filled the kettle with just the right amount of water. He then poured himself a glass of juice and got out his mum's favourite mug. If things went to plan, he'd be able to make his mum a cup of tea and still be leaving the house in five minutes.

As Femi waited, his mind drifted back to what his mum had told him last night about her latest visit to see Dr Patel.

He hadn't been able to sleep after that. In the end, he'd got up and played computer games until he finally fell asleep on the sofa.

"Good morning Femi," said his mum, shuffling into the kitchen.

Femi's mum had started to need a walking support to get around. Femi had noticed how recently she held on to the banisters with two hands when she went up and down the stairs.

"Would you like some toast, Mum?" asked Femi as he finished preparing her tea. "I've got time."

Femi knew his mum preferred to get her own breakfast, but he was already making toast anyway.

"I'm sorry if I upset you last night, Femi," said his mum.

Last night, when she'd told him that Dr Patel wanted her to start having visits from a carer, Femi had reacted badly.

Femi had told his mum that he could look after her, whatever happened.

"And that's what I told Dr Patel," his mum had reassured him. "So, nothing's going to change for now."

Femi had always helped his mum around the house, even before she got this horrible illness called MS. Everything had been fine then. But things were changing now. Only in small ways, but Femi noticed it. Like, how his mum was finding it harder to stand up by herself and how she found it difficult to put clothes on sometimes.

"These are all normal symptoms of multiple sclerosis," Dr Patel had told them the day she'd first visited them at home.

But what would happen if these 'normal' things got even worse?

Femi watched as his mum slowly lowered herself on to a kitchen chair. He handed her the mug of tea.

"We're coping with everything really well, aren't we?" said his mum.

"We're a team," said Femi, forcing a little smile.

"Good," said his mum firmly. "That's exactly what I told Mrs Wilde."

Mrs Wilde? What was his mum doing talking to his headteacher? Femi was about to ask when his toast popped up. As he quickly spread butter on it, Femi noticed how his mum carefully wrapped both hands around her mug so that she could drink the tea without spilling any. A few months ago, she would have used the handle.

"Now, go and have a great day with all your friends," she said. "Don't worry about me."

His mum's words were still ringing in his head as Femi hurried out of the house. Having a great day with his friends and not worrying about his mum were the two things Femi found most difficult. Just recently, he was feeling like he shouldn't go to school and leave his mum at all.

As he ran up the road, Femi passed a younger boy walking to school with his mum. *Me and my mum used to do that,* he thought.

It was hard to imagine walking anywhere with Mum now. A flood of memories came rushing back but he pushed them away.

Then, Femi spotted Carter up ahead and slowed down. He didn't want to catch him up. While he watched Carter getting further away, he wondered why it was so hard to get on with his friends these days.

If things carried on as they were, he probably wouldn't have any friends at all by the time he started secondary school. But if Carter, Lexi and Sara weren't going to be his friends any more, who would?

When Femi got to Greenwicks Primary, his friends
were too wrapped up in their football game
to even notice he was there. He went to sit by
himself at the foot of his favourite tree. As he
watched his friends play and have fun together,
Femi felt sad that he'd never liked ball games
enough to join in. But he hadn't ever told
them that.

"Carter, pass!" Lexi was shouting as she bounded
across the playground.

Femi saw Carter skilfully aim his pass for Lexi to
run on to. The half-deflated ball landed with a
bounce-less thud, right in Lexi's path. She kicked
it first time, straight between the two piles of
bags the friends were using as the goal.

"Goal!" cheered Lexi, doing her cartwheel celebration. When she landed, she stretched out her arms and pointed to the sky.

It was Monday morning. Some pupils were still arriving, but many were taking the chance to squeeze in some extra play before the doors opened. In his lonely spot by the tree, Femi's eyes drifted to the ant by his shoe. But he couldn't quite block out the sound of his friends having fun.

"You need to work on your celebration," said Sara, raising her hands like Lexi had done while wiggling her hips.

"Yeah!" laughed Carter, sticking his thumb into his mouth and rolling around on the floor.

The three friends collapsed with laughter as some of the younger kids started to copy them and make up funny celebrations of their own.

"Hey, where's Femi?" Sara asked, peering around.

Femi heard his name but didn't look up. The sound of his friends messing around seemed to be coming from another world. He sometimes slipped into that world on a good day, when he felt like he belonged there. But today didn't feel like one of those days.

"Hey, Femi, stop being such a misery-guts and come and play!" Carter called when he saw his friend.

Femi gritted his teeth and imagined Carter was the ant that was crawling over his shoe.

Femi was just about to flick the ant away but then felt sorry for the tiny insect and carefully shook it off.

"Femi's all right," Femi heard Lexi say to the others. "Leave him alone."

"He just doesn't like football," Sara replied. "You know that."

"Well, I tried to walk to school with him on Friday and he didn't say a word," said Carter loudly, clearly wanting Femi to hear. "I just don't think he likes hanging out with us any more."

Femi remembered that walk to school. Carter had gone on and on about how his favourite football team had lost two-nil in their latest match when they really should have won.

I mean, he knows I don't like football, Femi thought to himself now. *But he didn't stop talking about it, as if I might actually care!*

Just then, Mrs Coats opened the school doors and the children ran for their bags. Within seconds, the only evidence there had been a football match was the punctured ball left behind. Femi was the last person in the playground to head inside, and kicked the ball over the fence into the litter and weeds. He did a little celebration of his own before he headed to the library.

First thing on Monday mornings, Femi and his reading group had a five-minute slot in the library to change their reading books.

"What's up?" Sara asked Femi when she saw him staring at an empty shelf. Femi shrugged. He just didn't seem to be able to concentrate on reading any more.

"Hey, this one looks good for you, Femi," said Lexi, picking out a book about coding. "You're into computers, right?"

Again, Femi shrugged. He knew Lexi was trying to be friendly, but somehow he found her comment annoying.

She thinks she knows me just because she remembered I like computers, he thought to himself. *But really she hardly knows me at all.*

"Cheer up, Femi," said Carter. "It might never happen."

Something about Carter's teasing made Femi snap.

"Shut up," he muttered.

"No, you shut up!" Carter replied.

Femi clenched his fists and tried to shove his feelings back down fast.

"Calm down, Carter," said Lexi. "Femi hasn't said anything all morning and you're telling him to stop talking!"

For a moment, Femi thought Lexi's comment might have stopped Carter from saying anything else, but then ...

"I don't know what his problem is," Carter insisted. "He never wants to come to the park, play football or anything else. He's a big misery-guts!"

"I'm NOT a misery-guts!" Femi yelled, his feelings rushing out of him like a flood.

The whole library fell quiet. The only sound came from Carter, who was struggling to hold in a laugh.

"Just back off and leave me alone!" Femi shouted at him.

Carter's laugh finally burst from his mouth, so loud that it filled the room. Femi slapped his hands over his ears.

Femi's mum had told him to have a great day with his friends. She had no idea how difficult that was.

What friends? Femi thought to himself as he stormed out of the library.

2 Treasure Seekers

Femi was angry at himself for letting his rage erupt in the library. He tried to focus on what was happening in the classroom now. Mr Ali was pointing at a computer game on the screen.

"Our new maths game for this term is called Treasure Seekers," he announced.

Femi was normally happy when Mr Ali handed out laptops and headphones in class. But after his late night playing his computer game, he just couldn't stop yawning.

"Your first task will be to create an avatar," Mr Ali went on. "That's a virtual character that you can become within the game."

"Can I be a robot with laser eyes?" Carter called out, swinging back on his chair.

"You can be anything you want, Carter," said Mr Ali.

"Can I be a pink guinea pig?" Lexi called out. "A pink guinea pig who can dance and sing and fly like a duck?"

"Random," giggled Meena, loud enough for half the class to hear.

Mr Ali took a deep breath.

"You can be a badger in a tutu who can tap-dance and play the didgeridoo for all I care, Lexi. As long as you use the algebra and other maths I've been teaching you this term." he replied.

But Femi was smiling. He loved computer games, although he knew his mum worried that he spent too much time on them.

Femi watched keenly while Mr Ali pointed at the whiteboard and showed them how to start creating their avatars.

Femi got to work creating his avatar. The red-eyed zombie he ended up with looked exactly how he felt today.

"Once you've created your avatar, it might be fun to keep it a secret," Mr Ali said. "Each player scores points by using their maths skills to move their avatar through the game and collect treasure. And when your avatar finds some treasure, it's banked in your treasure chest."

"This actually sounds quite good!" Lexi exclaimed.

Femi agreed.

"*However*," Mr Ali said, then he paused and smiled, "at any point in the game, your avatars can meet up and work together with other players." Several pairs of eyes in the class shot around, looking for possible partners.

Mr Ali continued, "If you work as a team, you'll probably be able to find more treasure. Then you can split it between you. But some of you might prefer working on your own. So think about it. Are you a team player or a lone wolf?"

Lexi tried to howl like a wolf. It sounded more like a ghost, but it made everyone laugh, even Femi.

The room was filled with a buzz of whispering and chattering as everyone discussed how they planned to play the game.

Femi couldn't wait to get started. He looked at his zombie avatar again and made a few quick tweaks to its colour and features. Then he created a zombie name – Kraal 111 – and launched his monster into the game.

It wasn't long before Kraal 111 had unlocked a secret room in the Dark Lord's Palace and banked ten treasure chest points.

Femi was just studying his game map and deciding where to head next when he heard a sound from the other side of the classroom.

"Yesss!" Carter exclaimed. He'd just scored his first ten points.

Femi turned and saw a determined look on Carter's face.

Femi gritted his teeth. He wanted to win this game, and he definitely didn't want Carter to beat him!

Soon, Femi had banked his next ten points and was guiding his avatar through a barren valley, searching for more treasure. Then he spotted a ferocious-looking one-eyed dinosaur before it vanished behind a large boulder. Femi ran his cursor over the boulder and discovered that the beast hiding there was called Dino-Clops.

Was the Dino-Clops character a trap set by the game or was it another player? Femi jerked his head up to look around and saw Carter's screwed-up face as he played. Surely Dino-Clops had to be Carter's avatar?

I'm watching you, thought Femi as he stared at Carter.

Carter suddenly looked up and met Femi's eyes.

"Femi ..." muttered Carter.

"Everything all right?" asked Mr Ali quietly, looking up from his laptop.

Femi and Carter both looked down and threw themselves back into the game.

If Carter thinks he can beat me, he's in for a shock, thought Femi. He began typing instructions so fast and hard into his keyboard that it sounded like the stampede of a thousand scuttling beetles.

Femi was soon so lost in the game, he was thinking of nothing else.

For the first time all morning, he wasn't worrying about his friends, secondary school or even his mum. In the game at least, Femi had found a place he belonged and could have fun. *I'm a lone wolf*, thought Femi. *I don't care!*

Femi found a single gold coin lying on the ground by a huge rock and quickly banked it. He moved his avatar on towards Bandit Ridge and then stopped in horror. The Dino-Clops beast he'd seen before had just found twenty-five more pieces of gold by moving the huge rock where Femi's avatar had just been.

No! thought Femi, his eyes shooting to Carter, who was too engrossed in the game to look up. *That's twenty-five points!*

"Right, everyone – time's up," said Mr Ali. "But don't worry, this Treasure Seekers game is your homework for this week."

Mr Ali logged everyone out of the game, with many of the pupils groaning and throwing up their hands.

Mr Ali was looking at his screen. "Let me tell you, we do have a leader already – the avatar known as Dino-Clops."

"That's Femi, I bet!" Carter groaned, trying to tease Femi into admitting it.

If anyone's got that sneaky Dino-Clops avatar, it's Carter! thought Femi to himself. *He's just trying to put me off by pretending it's not him.*

"In second place, very close behind Dino-Clops, we have Kraal 111," Mr Ali continued. "With Rocket Man in third place."

Femi stopped listening. He was already planning how he was going to win this game. At least he could feel good about that, if nothing else.

As they stepped outside at breaktime, Carter grumbled to Femi, "You followed me and took treasure that should have been mine."

"No, I didn't," said Femi, his fury beginning to bubble inside again. "That's what *you* did to me!"

"Liar!" said Carter.

"It's only a game," said Sara, trying to calm the boys down.

And for the second time that day, Femi stormed off to be on his own.

Femi could hear his friends squabbling as he sank down under his usual tree. He closed his eyes and thought about the Treasure Seekers game. Gradually their voices faded away.

That night, Femi helped his mum make an omelette for them both and they sat down to eat at the kitchen table.

"Femi, you haven't told me how your friends are recently," said his mum, taking him by surprise.

Femi swallowed a bite of omelette. "They're all right," he said flatly.

His mum reached out to touch his hand and looked into his eyes.

"Femi, you have told them that you help look after me sometimes, haven't you?" she said. He noticed that her eyes were a little watery. "Good friends need to know these things."

"They know," Femi mumbled and pulled his hand away.

After he'd finished washing up, Femi logged into the Treasure Seekers game. He liked the way his worries slipped away as he lost himself in the game.

Femi played the game without stopping for a couple of hours before he heard his mum calling from upstairs.

"Coming!" he called several times before he actually moved. He realised he had pins and needles in his legs from sitting in one position for so long.

Femi felt frustrated having to log out of the game to help his mum get ready for bed.

"Would you like me to read to you, Femi?" his mum asked when she was comfortable. "Like I used to?"

Femi used to love his mum reading books to him when he was younger. Back then it had been Mum putting him to bed, not the other way round.

"Maybe tomorrow," said Femi. He didn't want to read books now. He wanted to get back to the game and get ahead.

"Promise me you won't stay up too late," said his mum, her face crinkling into a worried frown. He nodded.

Remembering her words, Femi tried not to look at the time when he finally crawled into bed that night, but he knew it was late. Much, much too late.

3 Falling ...

The next morning, Femi felt really tired. But he still made sure the first thing he did was check his ranking in the Treasure Seekers game. Kraal 111 was in the lead now, but not by much because Carter's Dino-Clops was only fifteen points behind.

"I'll have to play it for longer tonight," he sighed to himself as he headed to the kitchen to make his breakfast. "I'm not going to get beaten."

Femi was just pouring his cereal when he heard his mum call out to him from the hall. He found her sitting on the stairs.

"Mum?" he gasped.

"I tried coming down step by step on my bottom," his mum explained. "It was fine but now I'm finding it quite hard to stand up. I must be more tired than I thought."

27

Femi helped his mum up so she could get to her walking support.

"I could stay off school and help you today," said Femi. "We've got some maths homework. I could do some of that."

As soon as he said it, Femi felt guilty. His thoughts were bouncing around in his head. Did he really want to stay home to help his mum or so that he could spend more hours on the computer playing Treasure Seekers? He wanted both. But which one did he want more?

"Thank you, Femi," said Mum. "But going to school is important. Not just for your education, but so that you spend time with your friends. Don't worry, Dr Patel is coming to see me this morning and this afternoon my old friend Samira is popping round, so I've got lots going on."

Femi trudged to school, lost in his thoughts.

He didn't like the idea of Dr Patel coming to the house. A doctor coming to the house meant something was wrong. But things weren't that bad, were they? He and his mum were happy.

Why couldn't the doctor just leave them alone?

Femi was staring at the pavement, lost in his thoughts as he walked, when his three friends appeared alongside him.

"Hey!" panted Sara.

Femi winced and looked up.

"How are you?" gasped Lexi.

Femi tried to smile but he couldn't.

"Still not talking to us then?" said Sara.

"He's fed up because his stupid one-eyed Dino-Clops isn't ahead on the Treasure Seekers scoreboard!" said Carter. "I checked the scores this morning and that zombie thing is just ahead."

Lexi laughed and started dragging her feet across the floor. "Braaaaains ..." she moaned like a hungry zombie.

Carter and Sara were both laughing now, too.

"The thing that gets me," said Carter. "Is that I spent an hour on that game last night and I'm still back in third place behind both of them."

Femi really wished he could just tell Carter to grow up and not lie about the game. It was obvious that Carter was Dino-Clops, why didn't he just admit it?

That morning in class, Femi was far too tired to care about Mr Ali's grammar lesson. He could hear his teacher explaining something but his eyelids kept closing. They felt so heavy ...

Then a voice yelled, "Look out! He's going to fall!"

Femi jerked awake with a snort.

Femi's classmates roared with laughter. He realised with horror that he'd been asleep and almost fallen out of his chair.

"Sorry," he mumbled, staring down at the table in front of him.

"All right, everyone, calm down," said Mr Ali. "Let's get back to these imperative verbs."

"Are these kinds of verbs *really* that important, Mr Ali?" groaned Lexi.

"Because it's quite hard for some of us to keep awake," said Meena with a giggle. The class erupted again with another howl of laughter.

Mr Ali rolled his eyes and smiled. "Without imperative verbs, I wouldn't be able to tell you lot what to do," he said. "That's what makes them so important."

"And it's important not to fall asleep in lessons," said Leon.

"True, Leon," said Mr Ali. "But it's also important to listen to me."

Femi buried his head in his hands. If only he could just disappear into a computer game – he wanted to be anywhere but in the classroom now.

After the lesson, everyone forgot about imperative verbs. But they remembered Femi falling asleep and kept making jokes. When Mr Ali let them out for break, he asked Femi to stay behind.

"Femi, I know you have a lot going on at the moment," said Mr Ali gently. "And I want you to know that the school understands. We want to help both you and your mum."

Femi hated the fact that his mum and Mr Ali had spoken on the phone. But he knew that Mr Ali was only being kind. As Femi headed out to the playground, he found that he was crying.

That lunchtime, Femi stood in the lunch queue deciding what to eat, even though he wasn't hungry. When he heard his name, his ears pricked up.

"I don't think Femi wants to be friends with us," Lexi was saying. "It's obvious."

Femi peered around. His friends were talking about him. They were a few places behind him in the line, clearly with no idea he was there.

"And he's totally obsessed with that computer game!" said Carter.

"*You're* obsessed with it," Lexi objected. "Femi doesn't go on about it all the time."

Hearing his friends talking about him behind his back made Femi feel small, like an ant.

"If I had all the treasure that his annoying, one-eyed avatar has got, I'd be happy," Carter went on. "But Femi's never happy. He's more weird and miserable now than ever!"

Femi felt his fists start to clench.

"Does he ever do anything else apart from play that game?" Carter kept going on.

Femi started to shake. His feelings bubbled up inside until finally, he couldn't bear it any more.

"Shut up!" he yelled, stepping out of the line and turning to them. "Shut up! Shut up!"

"Whoops!" muttered Lexi.

Femi saw the shock on their faces and clammed up. He wanted to shout at them. He wanted to tell them how angry and upset it made him feel that they talked about him behind his back. If only they knew a tiny fraction of what it was like to be him, they wouldn't say the things they said.

Femi wanted to say these things but he couldn't. Instead, he let out a roar of frustration and stormed out of the hall.

4 Home

After his meltdown in the hall, Femi didn't want to be found. He headed straight through the playground and out on to the school field. In the far corner, not far from the back fence, there was an old oak tree with a thick trunk. Femi sat behind it and buried his head into his hands.

"Hey, Femi," said a quiet voice.

Femi looked up and saw Sara, peering around the trunk.

"We're sorry," said another voice just before Lexi's face appeared, too.

Then another figure leapt out and made Femi jump.

"Surprise!" cheered Carter.

"Go away!" snapped Femi, hugging his knees.

Femi could see that his three friends looked upset and confused by his reaction but he didn't want to feel sorry for them. They'd hurt *his* feelings, not the other way around.

"Come and hang out with us," said Sara.

"We could play football," Carter burst out.

"Femi doesn't like football," Sara reminded Carter.

Hello, thought Femi. *I am here, you know.*

He returned to staring at the ground. He was too tired to do anything, even if he'd wanted to.

"I think Femi just wants to be alone," said Sara after an awkward silence.

"Then meet us at the park after school," said Lexi. "We could hang out on the swings. Or we could climb that tree that looks over the houses on Green Lane."

"The lady at number forty-two has a llama," said Sara, raising her eyebrows and grinning. "Seriously, I've seen it."

"You're kidding!" said Carter.

Femi couldn't understand how they could be so normal and nice after his big blow-up. A part of him really wanted to say yes and go to the park with them.

"I can't," he said at last, remembering that he had to go shopping later.

As his friends walked off, Femi heard Lexi's voice. "Well, that didn't go very well."

Femi couldn't wait to get home that afternoon.

As soon as he got in, he told his mum he needed to get on with his homework before he did anything else.

An hour and a half later, Femi was still lost in the Treasure Seekers game. To his irritation, he was disturbed by a knock at the front door.

He opened the door and gasped. "Carter! What are you doing here?"

"I don't care about playing football," said Carter. "I just want you to come to the park so everything can be normal again."

Femi opened his mouth to reply but realised his friend was staring at something in the hall behind him.

"What's that?" said Carter, pointing.

Femi felt his face go hot.

"It's my mum's new walking frame," he mumbled.

Carter frowned, clearly confused.

"Who is it?" his mum called from inside the kitchen.

"It's only Carter," said Femi. "He's just going."

"Hello Mrs Okoro," Carter called.

"Well Carter, come in!" his mum said cheerily.

Femi saw Carter's eyes light up and he stepped forwards but Femi shook his head firmly. "I'm busy. Sorry." He started to shut the door.

Carter shrugged. "Okay. We'll be at the park if you change your mind."

"You're welcome here any time, Carter," called Femi's mum. "You and all Femi's friends."

Femi quickly closed the door in Carter's bewildered face.

"Femi," his mum said gently. "Do we need to talk?"

"Not now," called Femi, turning away from the kitchen door. "I've got to finish my homework."

Femi went straight back to the computer.

He was frustrated to see that even after all his work, Kraal 111 was stuck in second place behind that annoying Dino-Clops avatar. For another half an hour, Femi was so engrossed in the game he forgot that he needed to pop to the shop to buy some food for that evening. In the end, his mum had to come in and remind him.

"I'm feeling a bit dizzy, Femi," she said, leaning against the door frame. "Can you get the shopping now so we can eat soon?"

Femi's mum shakily lowered herself on to the sofa as he jumped up. He fetched the shopping list and bags from the kitchen. Then he headed out, lost in thought about what he would do next in the game.

5 Panic

Femi was trudging back through the park carrying his shopping with his head lost in the Treasure Seekers world when he saw his friends. He was about to turn and walk another way when he realised they were all stroking a dog.

"Hey, Femi!" Lexi called.

Femi wanted to drop the shopping bags and run as his three friends chased towards him with an excitable dog. He might have done it if the dog hadn't got to him so quickly.

41

"Down, Sandy!" shouted Lexi as the dog leapt up at Femi, her tail wagging frantically.

By the time the others had caught up, Femi was laughing and ruffling Sandy's head.

"Is she yours, Lexi?" he asked.

"Yeah!" gasped Lexi, clipping the dog back on to her lead.

Lexi went on, "We got her from the rescue centre just before my dad lost his job. I think it really cheers Dad up to take her out for walks. And she loves playing with me!"

The three friends were out of breath and panting almost as much as the dog.

Stroking Lexi's dog made Femi feel calmer than he had for a long time. Without thinking, he sat down on the grass with his friends and let her lick his face.

"She really likes *you*, Femi," said Lexi, grinning.

Femi couldn't help smiling as Sandy rested her head on his knee.

"She's really nice," he said. "I'd love a pet."

"We thought you weren't coming out," said Carter. "What's with all the shopping? Three bags is a lot!"

Femi looked over at the bags and realised how hungry his mum must be feeling by now. A familiar knotted feeling came back in his stomach.

"I'd better go," he said, avoiding Carter's question. "I need to cook."

"*You* need to cook?" said Carter. "What about your mum? Doesn't she do all the cooking?"

Femi felt prickly. He shouldn't have said anything about cooking. He felt like he'd been disloyal to his mum.

"Mum still cooks," he gabbled, quickly standing up with his bags. "But she finds it hard sometimes, so I help when I can."

"What do you mean?" asked Sara thoughtfully. "Is your mum ill?"

 43

Femi panicked and started to walk away. He'd let down his guard.

"Femi, you know you can tell us about it," said Sara. "Whatever it is."

"Maybe we could help you," called Lexi, as Femi hurried for home.

I'm such an idiot! Femi told himself. He screwed his eyes up and shook his head. His friends knew that something was wrong now. He didn't want to have to tell them about his mum's illness. He just wanted them to think he was normal.

Femi felt sick just thinking about talking to anyone about his worries.

As he headed out of the park, Femi grew more and more worried about his mum. What would happen if Dr Patel and his teachers thought that she couldn't take care of him any more? Where would she go? Where would *he* go?

Femi's arms were starting to ache from carrying the shopping bags so he sat down to rest at an empty bus stop.

A siren in the distance caught his attention. It got louder and louder before an ambulance went speeding past him. He watched it travel for half a mile or so up the road before it turned on to a street. That's when he realised ...

"Mum?" Femi panicked, leaving his bags and starting to run.

6 Changes

Femi was out of breath when he turned the corner into his street. At the very end of it, he could see the ambulance.

Femi pelted all the way down the street and in through the open front door.

"Mum!" he panted as he burst into the hall.

"Femi! I'm all right, don't panic," called a frail voice.

Then a paramedic stepped out of the living room.

"Your mum just got dizzy and had a little fall," he said kindly. "The doctor got here before us. Your mum's going to be fine. No harm done."

Femi followed the man into the room and saw his mum sitting up on the sofa with another paramedic and a doctor Femi recognised.

"Dr Patel?" Femi panted.

"Hi there, Femi," said Dr Patel. "I got your mum a couple of biscuits from the kitchen. She just needed to eat something. Come and sit with us."

"Dinner!" Femi cried out. "Mum needs food!"

Before anyone could stop him, Femi flew back out of the front door. How could he have been so stupid? This was ALL HIS FAULT! He'd played the Treasure Seekers game for so long he'd not even made her a cup of tea! What was he thinking of?

When Femi finally got back with all the shopping, the paramedics had gone. Dr Patel and his mum were talking in the kitchen but stopped the moment Femi walked in.

"I'm cooking beans on toast," Femi panted. "Don't worry, Dr Patel. Me and mum will be eating in five minutes. Honest."

Femi thought he caught a look between Dr Patel and his mum. He didn't like it.

"Femi," said Dr Patel. "Your mum falling is not your fault."

"But it is!" Femi burst out.

As soon as he said it, he wished he hadn't. He saw his mum's unhappy face and tried to calm down as Dr Patel said goodbye.

That evening, Femi made beans on toast for dinner while his mum sat at the table and played Nigerian music on her phone.

When Femi put the plates on the table and sat down, his mum put her hand on his. "You're an amazing person, Femi," she said. "None of this is fair on you or me."

Femi felt tears welling up and quickly rubbed his eyes.

"Femi, you are such a kind and caring boy," his mum went on. "I know you like to keep your thoughts and worries all to yourself, but it's good to talk about how you feel sometimes. I know you don't want to talk to me about your worries because you think I'll get upset. But I really wish you could."

Even the thought of talking about his feelings panicked Femi. He stayed quiet and took a gulp of water.

"And it's okay to want things for yourself, too," his mum added, squeezing his hand.

"I do want things for myself," said Femi. "I want you to get better so that everyone else will go away and leave us alone."

"That's not what I mean," said his mum.

Femi was quiet for a few moments.

"What do you mean?" he said, moving his beans around on the plate.

 49

"Like having friends around to hang out and talk with after school," she said. "Going to the park and having fun. You are very kind and lovely to look after me the way you do, but I can still do most things for myself, you know."

"I know," mumbled Femi, forcing himself to eat a mouthful of toast.

He decided to tell his mum about Lexi's dog, Sandy. He wanted her to know he *had* been doing some normal things.

"You should ask Lexi to bring Sandy over some time," said his mum. "I'd love to meet her!"

"Yeah, maybe," said Femi.

His mum started to stand up and he grabbed the plates off the table.

"I'll wash up," he said. "Don't worry."

By the time Femi had finished all his jobs, he was exhausted. He tried to play Treasure Seekers after his mum had gone to bed but he couldn't focus.

In the end, he went upstairs and slipped under his duvet, too tired to even change into his pyjamas. But still Femi couldn't sleep. He tossed and turned for hours. His mum had fallen over. She could have been badly hurt. It was all his fault for forgetting the shopping. Maybe his mum really did need more help. Maybe he needed help too. But who could help him?

7 Here to Help

The next morning, Femi woke up with a clear idea in his head. It was going to be hard but he knew his mum was right. He had to face his biggest fear and start talking to people.

But as Femi hurried out of the house, just the sight of his friends waiting for him at the corner made him panic. He shoved the apple he was eating into his pocket.

"Are you all right?" Lexi burst out.

"We heard about your mum's fall," said Sara, her face full of concern.

"Your mum ... I was ..." Carter stumbled. "I was really worried when ..."

Femi wasn't used to seeing Carter lost for words.

"She's okay," he said. "But it was scary seeing the ambulance."

Femi realised he was talking about his mum with his friends for the first time. It felt weird. It was a part of his life he usually never spoke about to anyone.

"So how long have you been looking after her?" asked Sara.

Femi wasn't sure what to say. He and his mum had always been a team, taking care of each other.

"I don't look after her," he said. "Not really. I mean, taking out the rubbish and cooking stuff is normal, right? And doing the washing?"

"I don't do any of that stuff," said Carter. "I have to clear the plates away sometimes."

"I don't do that stuff either," said Lexi. "I have to tidy my room and stuff, but not cooking and washing."

"Me too," said Sara.

Femi knew his life wasn't normal. But hearing his friends talk made him feel so different to them. He didn't want to be different any more. But he didn't want to keep hiding things either.

"I think my mum's going to need a bit more help than that now," Femi mumbled. "More than what I can do."

"If she needs a mobility scooter, my uncle's got a really cool one," said Lexi. "He loves it! And do you remember Fozia, the girl who used to come to our school? She used a wheelchair and now she's a professional athlete. She's got medals and a massive following on YouTube!"

Femi knew his friends were trying to be helpful, but they didn't really get it.

"I'm scared," he said quietly. "I'm scared things are going to have to change now and I don't know what that means. I mean, what if Mum has to go into a care home?"

Femi looked down and swallowed. "When would I see her? And what would happen to me? Would I have to go and live with my aunty?"

"No!" shouted Lexi and Sara together.

"You can't move away" exclaimed Carter. "That's even worse than going to a different secondary school!"

No one spoke for a few moments.

"And ..." said Femi, "... these last few weeks have been really hard for me, too. Do you think I should speak to one of the teachers and ask for some help?"

The others all nodded.

"We'll come with you," said Carter. "It's not fair that you have to do all that shopping and cooking all by yourself."

"We're here for you, Femi," said Lexi. "Whenever you need us."

"Always," said Sara.

Their headteacher was standing at the main gates as usual when Femi and his friends arrived at school.

"Mrs Wilde," said Femi nervously, standing in front of her. He was surrounded by his friends and Lexi slipped her arm through his. He cleared his throat.

"I need to talk to you today. Please ..."
Femi finished.

"Absolutely!" said Mrs Wilde with a smile. "Can we meet straight after afternoon register? I need to make a few calls this morning."

When Femi went to Mrs Wilde's office that afternoon, he felt so nervous he wasn't sure if he could go through with his plan.

"Femi – you're here!" said Mrs Wilde cheerfully when she saw him. "I've just been speaking with your mum on the phone."

When Femi stepped inside Mrs Wilde's office, he was shocked to see a smiley woman wearing a colourful jumper sitting on one of the soft chairs inside. She waved to him.

"This is Helen," said Mrs Wilde. "She's a therapist – someone you can talk to."

Femi felt a lump in his throat and his palms began to sweat. He glanced at Helen as she stood up to greet him and then stared at the floor. Could he just leave now?

"Helen's here to help you, Femi," Mrs Wilde went on. "And she can help everyone at school to support you, too."

"Your mum says you love computer games," Helen said. "She says they are something you're really good at. Maybe we could start with you telling me about your favourite game?"

Femi shrugged. When had Helen been talking to his mum? He didn't want to talk about his feelings now. Perhaps he should just say he felt sick and rush to the toilet?

"Come on," said Helen, putting her hand on Femi's shoulder. "Let's go and sit in a quiet room for a chat."

Femi felt his nerves slowly disappear as he sat and talked to Helen. She was so friendly, she made it really easy for him to open up about his feelings.

"Let's do this again soon," Helen said at the end of the session. Femi nodded happily.

When he got home, Femi told his mum everything about his meeting with Helen. Then they talked about the changes that his mum and Dr Patel were planning. Carers were going to start coming to help her two times a day.

When they were done talking, Femi helped his mum get ready for bed and found a book they used to read together.

"Can we read this again?" he asked, jumping on to the bed and sitting next to her.

That night, Femi and his mum sat and read and chatted for ages. He forgot all about the

 59

computer game. Who cared who was in the lead? When they were finally done, Femi went to his room, put on his pyjamas and fell straight to sleep.

The next morning, Femi found his friends waiting for him on the corner as usual. They all had worried expressions on their faces.

"Just tell us what's happening," Carter pleaded as they began their walk to school. "Are you leaving? Will we only be able to chat online now?"

"No! Everything's okay," said Femi, the tightness inside him gone now. "Some carers are going to come to the house to help Mum, so I don't have to do so much."

"So, you're not moving to your aunt's?" said Carter, holding up his hand to stop Femi talking.

Femi laughed.

"No, I'm not," he said. "And now I'll have more time to hang out with you."

"That's great news," Lexi said, gently punching Femi's shoulder. "We've missed you!"

Femi grinned and glanced up at his friends.

"Also," said Femi, deciding to open up a bit more. "That woman called Helen is going to see me in school so I can talk to her about things. She's going to come every week now."

"So, does this mean you can come back to my house after school and play Treasure Seekers sometimes?" said Carter. "Even if you are that annoying one-eyed Dino-Clops thing!"

Sara and Lexi both glanced at each other, then burst out laughing.

"Carter, you're just so easy to wind up!" Lexi howled.

Lexi had to stop giggling before she went on. "That silly one-eyed Dino-Clops thing is me! I should have told you, but I was having such a laugh winding you up!"

"What?" exclaimed Carter, in complete disbelief. "You? But you're actually doing all right. I thought you didn't even like maths!"

"I don't mind maths when it's in a game," said Lexi. "And when I teamed up with Sara, I did even better!"

Sara snorted with laughter and Lexi pulled a funny face.

Femi smiled, pleased for his friends. "Maybe working as a team is better?" he said.

"Well?" said Carter to Femi. "Are you coming back to my house today or not?"

"Or you could all come back to mine?" said Sara.

"Or mine?" said Lexi.

Femi felt a little tense. He could see how much his answer meant to them.

"Can we start with you all coming back to mine instead?" he asked.

Femi's friends beamed. "Yes!" they all said together.

"But can we do something else and not play Treasure Seekers?" Femi added. "I think I need a break from virtual worlds for a bit."

"Me too!" said Carter with a laugh.

"I could bring Sandy over?" Lexi said.

"I think my mum would love that," said Femi. He looked around at his smiling friends and grinned. He was back in the real world and it felt good.

Chat about the book

1 Who do we discover created the Dino-Clops avatar at the end of the story?

2 Go to page 39. 'Femi quickly closed the door in Carter's bewildered face.' What does 'bewildered' mean?

3 Why did Femi bury his head in his hands during the grammar lesson in Chapter 3?

4 Read pages 17–19. How do you know Femi enjoyed the computer lesson?

5 Go to page 34. How does the author show Femi's anger at this point in the story?

6 Go to page 24. Why do you think Mum said, "Femi, you haven't told me how your friends are recently"?

7 Why do you think the author chose 'Panic' as the title for Chapter 5?

8 Do you think Femi was right to describe himself as a 'lone wolf'? How would you have felt if you were in Femi's shoes?